## HOW'S SCH

Lizzie finds school is ju
thought it would be, and
friends to choose from there ~~~ ~~~ ~~~ dull moment.
There's Ranjit and Samantha, who both have red
anoraks just like Lizzie (which can be rather con-
fusing), Polly who gets wet twice when they go
swimming (and both times by mistake) and George,
whose wheelchair doesn't stop him causing as much
chaos as anyone! This is a lively collection of
stories about the ups and downs of the first year at
school.

Anne Rooke is an experienced playgroup leader,
and author of several books for children. She lives
in Canterbury, Kent.

# How's School, Lizzie?

## ANNE ROOKE

### Illustrated by Rachel Stevens

Lizzie Jones.

Here is Scruffy
Here is scruffy
in a space rocket.
in a space rocket.

PUFFIN BOOKS
in association with Blackie and Son Ltd

With thanks to
All Saints School, Chatham,
Bridge School
and Pilgrim's Way School, Canterbury

PUFFIN BOOKS

Published by the Penguin Group
Penguin Books Ltd, 27 Wrights Lane, London W8 5TZ, England
Penguin Books USA Inc., 375 Hudson Street, New York, New York 10014, USA
Penguin Books Australia Ltd, Ringwood, Victoria, Australia
Penguin Books Canada Ltd, 2801 John Street, Markham, Ontario, Canada L3R 1B4
Penguin Books (NZ) Ltd, 182–190 Wairau Road, Auckland 10, New Zealand

Penguin Books Ltd, Registered Offices: Harmondsworth, Middlesex, England

First published in two volumes by Blackie and Son Ltd 1990
Published in Puffin Books 1991
10 9 8 7 6 5 4 3 2 1

Text copyright © Anne Rooke, 1990
Illustrations copyright © Rachel Stevens, 1990
All rights reserved

The moral right of the author has been asserted

Printed in England by Clays Ltd, St Ives plc

# Contents

# How's School, Lizzie?

# 1 The First Visit

One morning Lizzie was sitting on her front doormat pretending it was a magic carpet when three letters landed on her head.

Lizzie jumped up and shouted, 'Hello!' through the letter box.

'Morning, Mischief,' the postman called back.

'I'll take these to Mum,' Lizzie shouted.

'You do that,' the postman agreed.

Lizzie's mum looked at the three envelopes and turned over the white one. 'This looks interesting,' she said. And a little later she added, 'Yes. It *is* interesting. It's about you, Lizzie. The school want you to go next Thursday to see what it's like. And, better still, they want both of us to stay to dinner. We'll have mince, carrots, potatoes, syrup sponge or fruit. How about that?'

'Good,' said Lizzie.

That evening Lizzie's dad read the letter too. 'Why aren't we asked along, Fred?' he said, picking up Lizzie's little brother. 'We like syrup sponge, don't we?' And Fred kicked his legs happily.

'Fred is going to Oliver's house. Mum said so,' Lizzie explained firmly. 'And, anyway, he's fat enough already.'

'Bad luck, Fred,' said Dad. 'No treats for you and me.'

And that gave Lizzie an idea.

Next Thursday morning, Lizzie and her mum walked along to the school.

'We're early,' said Mum, looking at her watch. 'Do you think this is someone else who's starting school today?'

Lizzie saw a small boy crossing the road towards the school and holding his father's hand.

'Good morning,' said the father. 'Shall we go in together?'

And he pushed open the heavy glass door of the school.

'Hello,' said a friendly lady from her office at the side of the entrance hall. 'You must be Ranjit and Lizzie. I'll take you along to Mrs Armstrong. She's expecting you.'

The kind lady led them down a corridor with coats hanging on either side. She stopped and knocked at an open door.

Lizzie saw a room full of busy children. Some were sitting at small tables drawing and writing. Some were building bricks in a corner. And Mrs Armstrong, the teacher, was helping three or four children to paint an enormous picture.

'Come in, Lizzie and Ranjit,' Mrs Armstrong said. 'Welcome to big school.'

'How do you do?' said Ranjit, just like a grown-up.

But Lizzie couldn't say anything at all.

Mrs Armstrong shook hands with the parents and then she turned to the children and smiled. 'Now, the first thing I do with all new children is to show them where the toilets are. Then you don't have to worry.'

So Lizzie and Ranjit followed Mrs Armstrong back down the corridor and stopped outside two doors.

'The blue door is the boy's toilet and the yellow door is the girl's toilet,' Mrs Armstrong explained. 'If you want to go in you knock first. If it's empty you go in. Do you want to, Lizzie?'

Lizzie nodded and dashed inside. Ranjit stayed put.

'And, do you see, Lizzie? The door shuts with a magnet, so you can't get locked in.'

'Good,' said Lizzie.

A little later, Lizzie and Ranjit went back to the classroom, and their parents went to have coffee with Miss Thompson, the head teacher.

'Would you like to explore the Wendy House, Lizzie and Ranjit?' asked Mrs Armstrong. 'There's lots to see.'

Lizzie found the Wendy House extremely interesting. She cooked real pretend potatoes on a real pretend stove while Ranjit cleared out the cupboards.

Suddenly Lizzie said, 'Are you five yet, Ranjit?' and turned to see what he was up to.

But Ranjit wasn't there.

Lizzie ran out into the classroom and looked around. There were two other boys with black straight hair like Ranjit's, but neither was in Ranjit's red jumper.

Just at that moment there was a loud yell from somewhere down the corridor. Mrs Armstrong ran to the door with Lizzie close behind her. 'What on earth was that?' she said. 'I'm sure it's coming from the teacher's room.'

She and Lizzie dashed down the

corridor and into the teacher's room. Lizzie looked across the low tables and newspapers to a door in the far corner.

'It's Ranjit,' Lizzie shouted above the din.

'But he's in the *teacher's* loo,' said Mrs Armstrong.

'Well, it has got a blue door too,' said Lizzie fairly.

At that moment Lizzie's mum, Ranjit's father, Miss Thompson and Mr Gann, the school caretaker, all arrived.

Ranjit's father ran to the toilet door. 'Be quiet, Ranjit,' he called. 'Just calm down and pull back the bolt.'

'I can't. I tried. It's stuck,' sobbed Ranjit and he began to cry again, louder than ever.

'I knew this would happen,' said Mr Gann, the caretaker. 'It'll be magnets on the teachers' doors next!' And he walked off towards the front door.

Lizzie ran after him. 'I'll help you,' she said.

Mr Gann got his oil can and walked around to where the little toilet window opened on to the playground. 'Now, young lady, I'll get a ladder and climb in,' he shouted above Ranjit's yells.

Lizzie shook her head. 'Don't you worry,' she said. 'Lift me up and *I'll* climb in. I've done it at home when we've forgotten the key.'

Ranjit's cries stopped in surprise as Lizzie's legs appeared through the window. Very carefully she slid on to the cistern and climbed down on to the toilet seat.

'Here's the oil can for the bolt,' called Mr Gann. 'I'll try to follow you if you need me.'

'Better not. You're probably too fat,' Lizzie called back, thinking about it.

But at that moment, Ranjit grasped the bolt, sniffed hard, and shot it back – just like that.

Lizzie and Ranjit walked out into the teacher's room and the grown-ups sat down in relief.

'Were you looking for your daddy, Ranjit?' Miss Thompson asked kindly.

'No. I was looking for the toilet,' said Ranjit.

'Is it dinner-time yet?' Lizzie asked.

'Nearly,' said Mrs Armstrong. 'Rescuing people is hungry work, isn't it, Lizzie?'

'Sometimes,' said Lizzie. 'But he rescued himself, really,' she added truthfully.

That evening Dad arrived home while Lizzie was watching television.

'How's the schoolgirl?' he asked.

'All right,' said Lizzie. Then she jumped up and pushed her hand into her trouser pocket. 'Shut your eyes,' she said. 'I've got a surprise for you.'

Dad stood with his eyes shut and his hand out.

'You can open them now,' said Lizzie happily.

Dad looked at the sticky, crumbly, fluffy piece of yellow mess Lizzie had

pressed into his hand and he began to laugh.

And that made Lizzie laugh too. 'It's syrup sponge,' she said. 'But please don't share it with Fred. He's rather fat already. And I really think,' she added sternly, 'that he might get stuck in the windows at school.'

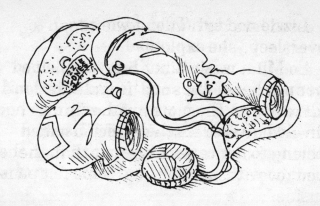

## 2 Muddles

Lizzie visited the school once more before the summer holidays began. She had her fifth birthday and went with her mum to buy a new school skirt and anorak.

She liked the anorak very much. It was blue with a red lining and had a secret pocket inside the zip.

At last the day before school arrived.

Lizzie had tea and said, 'I had better go to bed now.'

'Oh?' said Mum, wiping banana off Fred's face. 'It's only five o'clock.'

Lizzie nodded. 'I don't want to oversleep,' she explained.

So Mum washed her hair and helped her put her clothes on the end of her bed all ready for the morning. Lizzie also had an old battered satchel which used to belong to her cousin. She put that on the bed too with an apple and some felt pens inside.

By six o'clock she was tucked up in bed.

By seven o'clock she tried sleeping the wrong way round in her bed, but the clothes and satchel got in the way.

By eight o'clock she started to look at a picture book.

But by nine o'clock she went to sleep.

'It's as bad as Christmas Eve,' said Dad when he looked in on Lizzie before he went to bed.

Suddenly Lizzie woke up. 'School,' she thought as she sat up straight. 'Must get up. Lucky I put my socks and pants on last night. We mustn't be late.'

Quickly she pulled on her shirt, jumper and skirt and crept downstairs. Very quietly she opened the kitchen door and turned on the light.

'Woof!' barked Scruffy, the dog, rather surprised to see her.

'*Shsh*,' whispered Lizzie. 'We mustn't wake up Fred.'

But that bark was enough. Lizzie heard her parents' door open and Dad ran downstairs.

'Lizzie!' he said crossly. 'It's five o'clock. What are you doing?'

'Getting up in time,' Lizzie whispered. 'We mustn't be late.'

'Not much danger of that,' said her dad. 'Well, play with your Lego or something. But don't wake Fred.'

So Lizzie settled down to play until Mum came down to let out Scruffy and put the kettle on.

And yet, by the time their breakfast was over and Scruffy had been fed and Fred had been wiped down and stuffed in his push-chair, time was getting rather short.

'Look, shall I take Lizzie?' Dad said to Mum. 'You'll have to do the pick-up this afternoon.'

Mum nodded. 'It would help,' she said.

So, a little while later, Lizzie and Dad walked along to the school.

'Be good,' said Dad, kissing her goodbye.

'Good morning, Lizzie,' said Mrs Armstrong at the classroom door. 'Can you hang your coat on this peg with the picture of an aeroplane? That's right. Now, Ranjit. Your peg is the one with a red kite. Yes, good boy.' And so she went

on, making sure everybody knew what to do.

Slowly, all the children were shown to their places at the tables. Lizzie found she was sitting with Ranjit, Samantha, Polly, Joshua and George, who had a wheelchair.

Mrs Armstrong said, 'Now, children. You've all found your places so I'll read out the register. I'll call out your name and you each answer, "Here, Mrs Armstrong". All right?'

All the children answered Mrs Armstrong as she called their names and then she said, 'The next thing is our morning prayer for God's blessing on our day and to help us to be kind to each other.'

'Does it work?' asked Lizzie.

'Very often,' said Mrs Armstrong.

During the morning Lizzie drew a picture of Scruffy in a space rocket on the first page of her work book. Mrs Armstrong gave it a tick with her red pen and wrote 'Here is Scruffy in a space rocket' for

Lizzie Jones.

Here is Scruffy
Here is scruffy
in a space rocket.
in a z pace rocket.

Lizzie to copy underneath.

Later she said, 'It's quite windy outside today, children. So, if you want to get your coats, go and fetch them quietly now.'

Lizzie went along towards the pegs but found her anorak on the floor just in front of the toilet doors. She pulled it on and ran to the playground door.

'Have a good run about, children,' said Mrs Armstrong. 'But stand still at once when you hear the whistle.'

Lizzie ran along the edge of the playground with the wind behind her. Then she stopped and felt inside the secret pocket of her anorak. To her surprise there was something there. Lizzie pulled out a large chocolate biscuit wrapped in green foil. Mum must have put it there as a treat. Quickly she tore off the wrapping and began to eat the biscuit.

Then she felt in a side pocket and pulled out a crumpled handkerchief. Lizzie spread out the handkerchief and frowned. There was a picture of Winnie the Pooh. Lizzie knew the picture from her book at home. But she had never seen it on one of her handkerchiefs before. She blew her nose because the wind was making it run and stuffed the handkerchief back in her pocket, wondering if it was one of Fred's.

Just then the whistle blew and Lizzie stood still before running to line up at the classroom door. There she found Samantha in floods of tears. Mrs Armstrong was holding her hand and trying to comfort her. 'Now, tell me, dear,' Mrs Armstrong was saying, 'did your anorak have your name inside?'

Samantha nodded. 'My mum will be cross,' she said.

'What colour is it?' asked Mrs Armstrong.

'Blue with red inside,' said Samantha sniffing and looking in her sleeve for a handkerchief.

'Here,' said Lizzie, pulling out the Winnie the Pooh handkerchief, 'Use this.'

Samantha took it and blew her nose loudly. Then she looked at the handkerchief, and then she looked at Lizzie's anorak.

'That's mine. It's *all* mine!' she shouted, pointing at Lizzie.

'Hush, dear,' said Mrs Armstrong. Then she gently turned Lizzie round and looked inside the neck of her anorak. 'Yes. You're right, Samantha,' she said. 'Here's your name tape. "Samantha Barker", it says.'

Lizzie quickly pulled off the anorak and pushed it into Samantha's hands. Samantha stopped crying and began to smile. Lizzie dodged past her and ran to the peg with the picture of an aeroplane above it. There was nothing there.

'*Mine's* gone now!' she shouted.

'Oh, no,' said Mrs Armstrong walking over. 'There must be someone else with a blue and red anorak. But don't fuss, Lizzie. We'll find it.'

At that moment Samantha shouted,

'Someone's eaten my chocolate biscuit.'

Lizzie ran to her chair.

When everybody was sitting in their places again, Mrs Armstrong held up Samantha's anorak and said, 'How many of you have an anorak exactly like this?'

Lizzie, Samantha and Ranjit all put up their hands.

'Ranjit,' said Mrs Armstrong. 'Where have you put your anorak?'

'I've just put it back on the aeroplane peg,' said Ranjit.

'But I told you to put it on the peg with a picture of a kite – now didn't I?'

Ranjit nodded. 'But I found it on the aeroplane peg,' he explained.

'Children,' said Mrs Armstrong. 'You must all get used to using your own pegs and nobody else's. And do make sure your names are in all your clothes. All right?'

'Yes, Mrs Armstrong,' said all the children together.

At the end of the afternoon Lizzie saw Mum, Fred and Scruffy waiting for her in the playground.

She ran out and hugged them all.

'How did the day go?' Mum asked.

'All right,' said Lizzie cheerfully. 'And can I take a chocolate biscuit to school tomorrow? I want to give one to Samantha.'

'Oh?' said Mum in a surprised voice. 'Yes, of course. That would be a kind thing to do.'

'Yes,' agreed Lizzie pushing her hand into the secret pocket of her anorak and feeling the tiny teddy bear she had put there the night before. 'And I need my name in my coat – in case it gets muddled up. They do sometimes, you know.'

Mum sighed. 'Lizzie,' she said. 'I spent hours the other evening sewing name tapes into your clothes. Your anorak has your name, Lizzie Jones, at the neck. All right?'

'Good,' said Lizzie. 'I'll tell Samantha and Ranjit. They'll both have to learn to read my name.'

## 3 Swimming

'Mu-um,' Lizzie shouted as she ran across the playground at the end of school one day. 'Here's a letter for you. I've got nits.'

'Oh, no,' said Mum.

'Yes. Lots of them. Mrs Harper says so. Have you got nits?' Lizzie carried on.

But her mother was reading the letter and did not reply.

'Don't worry, dear,' said Joshua's

mother who was standing with her. 'Most of them get nits sometime or other. That lotion in the letter will get rid of them. No problem.'

'Well, I do hope so,' said Lizzie's mum in a worried voice. 'Come on, Liz. We'll go to the chemist *at once*.'

The next afternoon Lizzie rushed out of school holding another letter.

'What now?' said Mum. 'Worms – I suppose.'

'No,' said Lizzie. 'I don't think there are any worms. We're going swimming – all of us – next Tuesday.'

'Oh, good,' said Mum in relief. 'You'll enjoy that.'

That evening Lizzie heard a tap at the back door. It was Polly's mother – looking worried.

'Polly's in a real state,' she told Lizzie's mum. 'First she got all upset about having nits–'

'I didn't,' said Lizzie.

'—and now she's terrified about going

30

swimming,' Polly's mother went on. 'I don't know why, but she always has been.'

'Hmmm,' said Mum thoughtfully. 'How about going with her? The letter asked for parents to go too, if they could.'

'I'd have to cancel Tuesday morning work – and I'd have to take Ben,' said Polly's mother. 'But I think you're right. It ought to calm her down a bit.'

There were several parents waiting by the coach on the next Tuesday morning.

'Look, Polly,' said Lizzie in excitement. 'We're going on a real coach. Let's sit at

the back.'

'I'm sick in the back of buses,' said
Polly.

'But this is a coach,' said Lizzie.

But Polly sat in the front with her
mother and little brother Ben.

When the coach arrived at the swimming
pool the children and parents and
teachers were all shown into the school's
changing room.

'I've never been in here,' said Lizzie
looking round. 'It's good, isn't it?'

'No,' said Polly glumly. 'It smells.'

'That's the swimming pool. It always
smells like that,' Lizzie explained.

'It's horrid. Makes me feel sick,' said
Polly.

'Come along, Polly. Take off your shoes
and socks. See how quickly you can
change,' said her mother. 'Look at
George. He's nearly ready.'

At last all the children and parents had
changed into their swimming things. Mrs
Armstrong stayed in her clothes because

she had to walk around the edge of the pool making sure everybody was safe.

George was the first to flop into the water and the children watched as he streaked across the pool under water, his strong arms scooping the water back and his weak legs trailing along behind.

'He's good,' said Lizzie. 'I wish I could swim like that.'

'I don't,' said Polly as she stood,

miserable and shivering, wearing
armbands and Ben's blow-up ring around
her middle.

'Why don't you get in first?' Mrs
Armstrong whispered to Polly's mother.
'Then Polly might follow you.'

Polly's mother looked doubtful but she
lowered herself into the pool. 'It isn't cold
– aaah!' she added as Lizzie jumped in
beside her with a mighty splash. 'Well –
not very, anyhow.'

'I'll hold Ben's hand,' Polly said,
looking anxious. 'You have a swim.'

'Oh, very well,' said her mother,
beginning to swim gently across the pool.

'Wee-ee-ee,' yelled Samantha happily
as she ran and jumped into the water.
'It's lovely,' she shouted.

At that, Ben gave a sudden jerk. He
wrenched his little hand out of Polly's
and tottered towards the water. Without
a pause he stepped straight over the
ledge at the water's edge and dropped
into the pool. 'Wee-ee-glup,' he said as he
went down.

'Mummy! Help!' screamed Polly as she

rushed to the side of the pool just in time to see Ben's astonished face come bursting up to the surface of the water.

'Got you!' said Mr Ram as he swam strongly up behind Ben and lifted him up out of the water and plonked him down on the side of the pool.

'More! More!' shouted Ben in glee and stepped right back into the water again.

'Oh, no you don't, young man,' said Mr Ram gently lifting him out again. 'You wait until you've got armbands on. Then you'll be safe.'

'He liked it. He really liked it,' Polly said in amazement as her mother arrived in a breathless rush.

'I'll put him in those armbands and then he can really enjoy himself,' said Polly's mother.

Suddenly Mrs Armstrong blew her whistle. 'Time to get out, everybody,' she said. 'How time flies!'

'Oh,' said Polly happily. 'I haven't had a chance to get wet.'

'Better luck next time,' said Mr Ram.

Lizzie and Polly were the first to get changed. They rolled up their swimming things in their towels and waited leaning against the changing-room wall for the other children to finish dressing.

'What's that?' said Polly, pointing to a silver knob on the tiled wall just above their heads.

Lizzie looked. 'It says per-uh-sh,' she spelt out. 'What does that mean?'

'It means "push",' said Polly.

So Lizzie did.

And a torrent of water streamed down on Polly and Lizzie, drenching them in an instant.

'Children! Stop!' shouted Mrs Armstrong racing across the changing room and grabbing the children out from under the shower.

'Lizzie, that's the shower. Look at your clothes. You're soaked,' said Mrs Armstrong.

Lizzie watched the water drip down off her nose and on to the floor. 'Yes,' she agreed. 'I'm soaked.'

Polly shook the water out of her hair. 'So I did get wet, after all,' she said. 'And perhaps,' she added, her face lighting up, 'it'll wash out more nits.'

## 4 Brown Bread

One morning Lizzie went over to the
work trays under the classroom window.
She wanted to fetch her number work
book and colour in the nine grey
elephants she had drawn the day before.
She pulled out her tray and took out the
number book. As she did so she sniffed. A
horrible smell was coming from her work
tray.

Lizzie frowned and pushed her tray back in. She sniffed carefully but the smell had gone. Bending down she pulled the tray out again and, sure enough, the smell came out again too. Putting the tray down on the floor, Lizzie knelt and peered into the shadows at the back of the shelf. There was something there. She put her hand into the dark shelf and groped about. Her hand touched something hard. She pulled it out, and, 'Aah!' she shouted.

The whole class jumped.

'Lizzie! Whatever's the matter? Oh, good heavens!' said Mrs Armstrong.

Lizzie gazed at what she had dropped on the floor. It was a greenish-blue hairy thing – small and hard. 'It's a sandwich,' said Lizzie. 'A mouldy old sandwich.'

Mrs Armstrong looked at it too. 'Yes,' she said shortly. Then she pulled out Samantha's tray from beside Lizzie's and said, 'And there are plenty more where that came from.' And she sounded very cross.

Mrs Armstrong walked quickly over to

the cupboard and fetched the dustpan
and brush. The children sat very quietly.
They weren't used to seeing such a cross
Mrs Armstrong.

Briskly Mrs Armstrong swept the
remaining mouldy sandwiches into the
dustpan.

'Well,' she said. 'Who has been putting
their sandwiches behind the work trays?
If you own up at once I won't be cross.'
And as she said it Mrs Armstrong looked
hard at Samantha.

Samantha's face was red and her eyes
were filling with tears.

She took a deep breath and whispered,
'I did.'

Mrs Armstrong sighed. 'That was a
very naughty thing to do, Samantha. It's
unkind to your mother who made you
your sandwiches. It's caused a disgusting
smell and if food is left around the school
it encourages mice. But you're a good girl
to own up at once and I'm sure you'll
never do such a silly thing again. Now,
blow your nose and get a bucket of water
from the sink. We'll wipe the shelf down

PBROjTTHJii

with disinfectant.'

Samantha did as she was asked and the class carried on with the morning's work.

At dinner time Mrs Armstrong said, 'You've all worked very well and sensibly this morning. Good children.' And she walked along beside Samantha to the hall for dinner and sat down next to her.

Samantha opened her packed lunch box and sighed as she got out her sandwiches.

'What's the matter, dear?' Mrs

PD

Armstrong asked kindly. 'Why don't you like your sandwiches?'

'I don't like brown bread,' said Samantha. 'I like white bread.'

'But brown bread is better for you,' said Mrs Armstrong. 'That's why your mother gives it to you. Brown bread will make you grow up tall and strong.'

Samantha nodded and looked glumly at her sandwich. Then she took a great bite and sat staring straight ahead with her mouth full and not chewing at all.

'Don't be silly, Sammy,' said Mrs Armstrong, 'eat it up. I wish someone made me such good sandwiches.'

Slowly and crossly Samantha began to chew, but when Mrs Armstrong stood up to go and fetch her own dinner from the serving hatch, Samantha quickly wrapped up the remains of the sandwich and started eating her apple instead.

At going-home-time Mrs Armstrong beckoned to Samantha's mother through the classroom window. She came in and they spent a few moments talking together.

When Samantha's mother came out of the classroom she looked rather cross. 'Really, Samantha,' she said as they walked out of the school gates. 'What a silly thing to do. It just encourages mice – apart from anything else.'

The next day Samantha met Lizzie outside the classroom door.
     'Look,' she said, opening her packed

lunch box. Lizzie peered inside and saw two cheese sandwiches made of white bread.

'Good,' Lizzie said. 'You won't put those behind my tray, will you?'

And Samantha shook her head.


A few days later Mrs Armstrong had her apron on when the children came indoors from morning play. On her table she had a large mixing bowl and some packets.

'Now, children,' she said as they all sat down in their places. 'Today, because it's nearly Easter, we're going to make some hot cross buns.'

Mrs Armstrong pointed to the things on her table. 'We need yeast and currants, spice and margarine, warm water and – to make them extra good – brown sugar and brown flour. So I want you to wash your hands, a table at a time, and then fetch your aprons and sit down.'

George went round in his wheelchair with some packets on his lap and gave out a pile of currants to each table. Lizzie put a bowl of flour on each table, and

Harinder cut up the lump of yeast and put it in some warm water.

Everyone was kept very busy and Mrs Armstrong said she felt exhausted when, at last, four children carried the tins of hot cross buns off to Mrs Stewart in the kitchen to be baked.

The next morning Mrs Armstrong said, 'Well, children, did you enjoy your hot cross buns?'

'Yes, yes,' shouted the children. But Samantha said nothing.

'Did you enjoy yours, Samantha?' Mrs Armstrong asked.

Samantha shook her head.

'Did your mummy have it then?' Mrs Armstrong asked.

Again Samantha shook her head.

'Then who did have it?' said Mrs Armstrong.

Samantha folded her hands. 'Well,' she said. 'I put it in the cupboard under the sink where Mum keeps the washing up stuff.'

Mrs Armstrong frowned slightly.

'Why?' she asked.

'Because my brother Joe,' said Samantha, 'he wants a mouse, you see, for his birthday. And you said – and Mum said too – that brown bread encourages mice. So I thought I'd try with that bun. It might work – if I'm lucky.'

'Samantha,' said Mrs Armstrong firmly, 'when you get home you go straight to that cupboard and take out that bun, do you understand? What would your mother think if her kitchen

was overrun by mice?'

'But my brother Joe – he really wants a mouse – he does,' said Samantha sadly.

'Then your parents might get him one at a pet shop,' explained Mrs Armstrong. 'But in the meantime, they don't want buns going mouldy and giving them nasty shocks in cupboards, do they?'

'I know,' said Samantha. 'I'll wrap up that bun and give it to Joe instead. He likes brown bread. He won't mind.'

'That's an excellent idea,' agreed Mrs Armstrong. 'And now get out your reading book, Samantha. There's work to be done.'

# 5 Diwali

One wet morning Lizzie arrived at school just as Ranjit and his father were unloading some black bags from the back of their car.

'What's in those?' Lizzie asked.

'Things for Diwali,' said Ranjit.

'Oh,' said Lizzie. But she didn't know what he meant.

Just then Mrs Armstrong came out of

the classroom and called, 'Thank you, Mr Ram. I've been trying to get the Divali story straight in my head. But it's very complicated, I'm afraid.'

Ranjit's father smiled. 'Keep it simple,' he said. 'But don't miss out the monkeys.'

Later, when all the children had arrived, Mrs Armstrong said, 'We're trying something new today, children. We're going to act a story from India, where Ranjit's and Harinder's grandparents live. And, if it's good enough, we'll do it in assembly next Wednesday, so that all the school and your parents can see it too. How about that?'

The children were very excited and watched while Mrs Armstrong carefully lifted the things out of the black bags and hung some up around the walls.

There were silken cloaks and shining crowns, golden slippers with pointed toes curling upwards, brightly-coloured tunics with trousers to match, and, best of all, some masks.

Lizzie picked up one of the masks. It

was a bright red face with red paper streamers at the side and an extremely nasty expression. Lizzie loved it. She held it against her face and turned towards Mrs Armstrong.

'All right, Lizzie,' said Mrs Armstrong. 'You can be the devil Ravana.'

'*Thank you*,' shouted Lizzie through the terrible devil's mask.

'And now,' said Mrs Armstrong looking around thoughtfully, 'we need an old king to sit on the throne. How about you, Joshua? And he has three wives – two nice and one nasty. Who's clever enough to play the nasty one? That's the tricky part. All right, Samantha, you can try, but remember to speak in a really nasty voice.'

'Please, Mrs Armstrong,' said Ranjit, putting up his hand. 'Can I be Rama? He's sometimes called Ram and that's my name too.'

'Yes, all right,' agreed Mrs Armstrong. 'And who shall we have for Sita, your wife? How about you, Harinder? You could wear your beautiful sari.'

But Harinder shook her head. Shyly she put out her hand towards a monkey face mask. 'Can I be a monkey, please, Mrs Armstrong?' she asked quietly.

'Yes, of course, dear,' said Mrs Armstrong. 'And we want two more monkeys as well. No, not that many,' she added as nearly everybody shot up their hands. 'I can do without too many monkeys. I'll have James and Polly. They won't gibber too much.'

George was the best at talking out loud so he was the narrator and had to tell the story of Rama and Sita who were sent away into the forest for fourteen years and monkeys came to cheer them up.

'Do the monkeys stay in the forest for fourteen years too?' asked Polly looking worried.

'No, dear,' said Mrs Armstrong. 'You have to make yourselves scarce because Ravana, the terrible devil, is going to kidnap Sita and you don't want him to get you too.'

'I don't mind,' said Lizzie in a terribly nasty voice. 'I can get the monkeys too.'

'Stop it, Lizzie,' said Polly crossly.

'Yes, don't be too frightening, Lizzie,' said Mrs Armstrong.

'Anyway, Rama kills the devil at the end,' said Ranjit. 'Then he gets on his father's throne.'

'But what about me?' said Joshua. 'I'm the king. *I* sit on the throne.'

'Well, you do at first,' Ranjit explained. 'But then you die, I'm afraid.'

'Bad luck, Josh,' said Lizzie from behind her mask.

'Now, Lizzie,' said Mrs Armstrong sternly, 'that's enough. We'll let George tell the story and you just act your part, all right?'

'Yes,' said Lizzie in her normal voice.

That evening Dad helped Lizzie to wash her hair in the bath. He was just rubbing up the shampoo into a good lather when suddenly his hands stopped. 'Got them,' he said in a pleased voice.

'Got what?' asked Lizzie.

'Your horns.'

'What horns?' shouted Lizzie.

'Your devil's horns,' said Dad in a low voice. 'Mum said something about you becoming a devil, didn't she?'

Lizzie lay back in the water with a horrible grin.

'Aarh,' said Dad and pulled out the plug. 'There's only one way to deal with devils,' he said. 'You cast a spell and wash them down the drain!'

'No, no,' shouted Lizzie, jumping out of the bath and running, dripping into her bedroom. 'Come to school on Wednesday and you can see.'

Next Wednesday all the children and lots of parents crowded into the school hall.

The curtains were drawn and the hall was almost dark. Suddenly some Indian music sounded from the tape recorder, and just two lights went on.

George pushed his wheelchair to the front of the hall and said, 'Today we are telling the story of Divali, the Hindu Festival of Lights.'

All the children sat very still as Class Seven acted out the story of Rama and Sita.

Suddenly Lizzie bounded forward. With knees bent and feet wide apart she let out an ear-splitting yell, shaking her mask and trailing red streamers.

'*Aarh-aarh-aarh!*' came back an even louder shout from the middle of the audience.

Lizzie stopped in her tracks and peered through the eye-holes of her mask. Dimly she could see Fred screaming his head off with horror at this dreadful devil.

Lizzie sighed. She pulled the mask away from her face and shouted in her

normal voice, 'It's all right, Fred. It's only me.'

Fred stopped yelling at once and gazed back in astonishment.

The audience laughed and clapped loudly.

Lizzie put back her mask, spread her feet carefully and got on with the part.

At the end, six children came forward to welcome Rama home to his throne. They carried pots called divas with lighted candles inside. As they bowed to Rama a voice shouted, 'Look, sweeties!'

Lizzie looked up sharply. There was Fred standing on Dad's lap waving happily.

'That's right,' said Mrs Armstrong, carrying in a great tray loaded with white, yellow and brown sweets. 'Look what Mr Ram has made us all. They're special Divali sweets.'

Everybody clapped. Mr Ram smiled

and shrugged and said he had enjoyed doing it. The children passed around the fudgy sweets while the teachers lit candles at the sides of the hall and asked a grown-up to guard them for safety.

The next week Lizzie had the greatest surprise.

There, on the very front page of the local paper, was a picture of her – in the devil's mask.

'Can I cut it out and send it to Granny?' she asked at once.

'All right,' said Dad. 'She always said I was a little devil, so she won't be too shocked if you are too, will she?'

# Lizzie and Friends

# 1 The Green Fair

One afternoon Mrs Armstrong, the
teacher, said, 'We have an important day
coming up, children. Next week it will be
the school Autumn Fair. It's always a
lovely day but there's work to be done
first.'

'Good,' said Lizzie.

'That's the spirit,' said Mrs Armstrong. 'There are two things for you all to remember. Firstly; you can all come in fancy dress. The lady who reads the news on television is coming to open our Fair this year and she will judge all the fancy dresses first. It doesn't need to be anything fussy. Something quite simple will do. All right?'

'I can wear my brother's cowboy outfit,' said Joshua happily.

'And the second thing is this,' said Mrs Armstrong. 'Ask your mums and dads for something to sell on our stall. This year we'll have green things – not blue or yellow things but just green things. All right? Can you all remember that?'

'Yes, Mrs Armstrong,' said the children.

Ten days later it was the Saturday of the Autumn Fair.

'What shall I wear for my fancy dress?' Lizzie asked Dad.

Dad was grilling some sausages for their early lunch and gave one of the sausages a sudden jab. 'I'd forgotten

66

about that,' he said.

'Me too,' said Lizzie.

'Well,' said Dad, 'let me think. Yes, I know,' he said and darted out to the dustbins. He came back carrying two cardboard boxes. 'They've got a bit wet outside, but that can't be helped,' he said.

Quickly, Dad turned the larger box upside down and cut a hole in the bottom. 'The hole's for your head to go through,' he said. Then he reached for the thick blue marker pen and drew a huge clock face on the front of the box.

'What time shall I make it say?' he asked.

'Three o'clock,' said Lizzie.

'All right,' said Dad and he lifted the box over Lizzie's head and rested it on her shoulders. 'Now for the roof and a trap door for your face to look out,' he said.

Whistling happily, Dad cut the second box to make a roof shape. Then he plonked it over Lizzie's head.

'It's dark in here,' Lizzie shouted.

'Hang on,' said Dad as he cut a door in the cardboard in front of Lizzie's face. 'Now,' he said, opening the door. 'Stick your face out and say "Cuckoo". You're a cuckoo clock, you see.'

'Cuckoo,' said Lizzie as Mum dashed into the kitchen with Fred under one arm.

'What's burning?' she said.

Dad dived at the grill.

'Oh, really!' said Mum crossly as she looked at the burnt sausages.

'Can I go in my nurse's outfit?' Lizzie asked as the door of the clock shut all by itself.

'No!' shouted Mum and Dad together.

By half-past one Lizzie and her family
were standing in the school playground
with Ranjit and his family, waiting for
the television lady to start judging.

'What are you?' Ranjit asked Lizzie.

'A cuckoo clock,' said Lizzie. 'I have to
say "cuckoo, cuckoo",' she added glumly.
'What are you?' she said, looking hard at
Ranjit who was wrapped in white paper
with writing down the front.

'I'm a tube of toothpaste, of course,'
Ranjit said.

'Get ready, children,' said Lizzie's dad

69

in an excited voice. 'Here she comes.'

As the lady newsreader approached, Lizzie's clock door shut in her face.

'What's this little chap supposed to be?' said the lady.

Lizzie blew hard at the door to open it. It didn't budge. She butted it with her head desperately and suddenly it burst open and Lizzie's red face filled the doorway.

'Hello. It's a girl!' said the lady in a delighted voice.

'Quack-quack. Quack-quack. Quack-quack,' said Lizzie as the door gently swung shut again.

The lady passed on to Ranjit who explained about his red hat being the toothpaste cap and how he liked seeing the news on television.

Meanwhile Lizzie's dad yanked off the roof of the cuckoo clock. 'You show-off,' he said.

Lizzie giggled. 'Woof-woof-miaow,' she said.

'We might have won if you'd been a well-behaved cuckoo,' Dad said.

'Ducks are funnier,' said Lizzie. 'But it is a very nice clock,' she added kindly.

Suddenly they heard Miss Thompson's voice on the loudspeaker saying, 'And the winner in the Fives-and-Under section is Ranjit Ram – the tube of toothpaste.'

'Oh, well,' said Dad as he clapped for Ranjit. 'If only the sausages hadn't burnt I could have added a pendulum – and weights like pine cones.'

Lizzie nodded.

'Still, never mind,' Dad added, bracing up. Then he winked at Lizzie. 'Next year

you'll be tall enough to be a grandfather clock.'

Ranjit's and Lizzie's mothers were both helping during the afternoon on the green stall. There were lots of things for them to sell: plants and green vegetables, tinned peas and washing-up liquid, some green mugs and plates, books and beautiful, heart-shaped green peppermint creams made by Ranjit's mother.

On the ground in front of the stall there was a basket full of surprises wrapped in green tissue paper, all costing ten pence.

Lizzie and Ranjit took people's ten pences and handed them to their mothers. Then they watched the people unwrapping their presents.

Suddenly Lizzie said to Ranjit, 'My mum read me a story last night.'

Ranjit nodded.

'Well,' Lizzie went on. 'It was about some children who used to wrap up earth in brown paper parcels and leave them on the road outside their house for people to

pick up. And when they unwrapped them
they got a horrid shock – because it was
just messy old earth.'

Ranjit laughed.

Then Lizzie looked at the used bits of
tissue paper in the waste bin. And then
she looked at Ranjit and Ranjit looked at
her.

Grabbing up a handful of tissue, Lizzie
began to crawl off under the stall. 'Come
on, Ranjit,' she whispered.

Standing up, they raced around to the
back of the school where the class flower
beds lay in a neat line. They flopped down
beside the nearest one and Lizzie spread
out a small sheet of crumpled tissue and
filled it with a handful of earth.

'How do we do them up?' Ranjit asked.

'With lick,' said Lizzie. 'It might stick
like an envelope.'

'No, it doesn't,' she said a bit later. 'But
it'll have to do.'

'Let's take them back. Your mouth's all
green,' said Ranjit.

The children raced back around the
school carrying the little parcels and
crawled under the stall to their places by

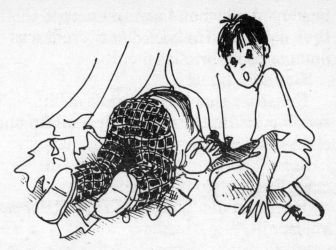

the basket.

'We mustn't sell them. That's bad,' said
Lizzie. 'We'll just give them away. Let's
try one out on Fred first. He's over there
by my dad with the hot dogs.'

Quickly, they ran over to Fred's
pushchair.

'Look, Fred,' Lizzie shouted. 'We've got
a lucky dip for you.'

And she pressed a sticky green parcel
into Fred's hand. Fred smiled happily
and untwisted the paper as all the earth
cascaded over his legs. He stared,
puzzled, at the mess he had made. Ranjit
and Lizzie laughed and laughed. But

Fred bent down and picked up a little brown pebble. He looked at it, sniffed it and popped it into his mouth.

'Oy,' said Lizzie.

'No, stop!' shouted Ranjit. 'You mustn't swallow it.' But Fred already had. And he opened his mouth wide to prove it.

Lizzie and Ranjit peered inside just in case. But the stone had gone.

'He might die,' said Lizzie in a stricken voice.

'Quick,' said Ranjit, feeling frightened. 'There's Harinder's father. He's a doctor. He might stop him.' And grabbing Fred's pushchair he rushed off while Lizzie ran, crying, to fetch Mum.

Harinder's father bent down and picked up Fred who was yelling loudly now that Lizzie and Ranjit were shouting so much. He listened to Ranjit and nodded. 'Was it a smooth stone?' he asked.

'Yes,' said Ranjit.

'How big?'

Ranjit thought. 'About the size of a baked bean,' he said.

'Well,' said Harinder's father handing Fred over to his worried mother. 'It will just come out when he goes to the toilet. So you mustn't worry, Mrs Jones. But you two children,' he said turning to Lizzie and Ranjit, 'you must remember that little children must not be given stones. They think they're sweets.'

Lizzie nodded unhappily. 'I expect he thought it was a peppermint,' she said.

'It wasn't green,' Ranjit argued.

'Either way,' said Lizzie's mum firmly, 'do be more careful in future.'

## 2 George's Laugh

One afternoon at school, Mrs Armstrong
said, 'Next week, children, we are going
to have a Theme Week. We have one
every year and it means that the whole
school finds out about one particular
thing. And this year we're going to learn
about Australia.'

Joshua shot up his hand at once.
'Kangaroos live in Australia,' he said.

'So does my uncle,' said Samantha.

'Does anyone know where Australia
is?' asked Mrs Armstrong.

'It's a long way away,' said Joshua.

'That's right,' said Mrs Armstrong. 'It's

a huge island right on the other side of
the world. So see what you can find out
about it over the weekend and on
Monday we'll start our great Australia
week.'

Over the weekend Lizzie's mum found a
book of colour photographs of Australia
and said she could take it to school. Lizzie
looked and looked at it and Mum read the
words under the photographs. Lizzie
could hardly wait to get to school on
Monday morning and when, after

prayers, the class sat down in the book corner, she waved it above her head to show Mrs Armstrong.

'What a beautiful book, Lizzie,' said Mrs Armstrong. 'Put it on the table and we'll look at it during the week. And what have you got, Joshua?'

'It's a boomerang,' Joshua explained, holding up a curved piece of wood. 'My brother made it for me and it's what people in Australia use for hunting. If you throw it it comes back. Only this one doesn't because my brother made it.'

'I see,' said Mrs Armstrong. 'What about you, George? What have you got in that plastic bag?'

'Nothing much,' said George and he began to wriggle about in his wheelchair.

'Oh?' said Mrs Armstrong suspiciously.

George began to laugh. 'It's just a picture of an Australian bird,' he said, pulling it out of the bag and handing it to Mrs Armstrong. 'It's a kookaburra. A laughing kookaburra,' he said and began to squirm about most strangely.

Mrs Armstrong turned the picture to face the class and they saw a bird sitting

on a branch with its beak open and its
feathers standing up on its head. But it
was no ordinary picture because the hills
behind the bird looked really far away
and the bird looked as if it was about to
fly out of the picture.

'What a wonderful effect,' said Mrs
Armstrong. 'I wonder how it's done.
Whatever's the matter, George?'

'Nothing,' said George in a stifled voice.
'But if you pull the string at the back
something will happen.'

'Oh?' said Mrs Armstrong and, very carefully, she pulled a short string which hung down behind.

'He-he-he,' went the picture – quietly at first.

Then, 'He-he-he-he-hahahaha,' went the picture.

George collapsed with laughter.

Mrs Armstrong's mouth began to curl.

'Ha-ha-ha-HE, HE, HE, HEeee —' went the bird, higher and higher and faster and faster.

The children began to laugh. Mrs Armstrong laughed too. George lay back in his wheelchair and flapped his arms helplessly.

Suddenly the Kookaburra stopped dead.

'Pull it again – please, Mrs Armstrong – please,' said Lizzie. So Mrs Armstrong pulled.

'He-he-he,' the picture began again and all the children began to shout and roll about with laughter.

Mrs Armstrong got out a tissue and wiped her eyes. 'Oh dear, oh dear,' she said. 'What a way to start a Monday

morning. George, I should have guessed you'd find something to drive us all silly. Yes, Miss Baxter?' she added as the teacher from the next door class put her head around the door.

'I wondered what all the noise was about,' said Miss Baxter.

Mrs Armstrong looked at George and they both giggled. Then Mrs Armstrong put on her serious face and said, 'George has got something very remarkable from Australia, Miss Baxter. And I really think he and Lizzie ought to take it round to show the other classes. They *will* be interested.'

Miss Baxter nodded and went back to her class and George and Lizzie set out with the kookaburra carefully done up once more inside the plastic bag.

'Where shall we go first?' Lizzie asked as they went down the corridor.

'Into Miss Baxter's, of course,' said George.

Miss Baxter's class was talking about the animals and birds of Australia, so Miss Baxter was very interested to hold George's picture for them all to see.

'Here's a kookaburra, children,' she said.
'It's sometimes called a laughing jackass.'

Lizzie nudged George. 'You tell her,'
she said.

'You have to pull the string at the
back, Miss Baxter,' George called out.
'That'll make it work.'

Miss Baxter peered at the string and
then tugged it briskly.

'He-he-he. He-he-he-hahahaha,'
rattled off the kookaburra as fast as a
rocket.

'Good heavens,' said Miss Baxter as the
bird began to scream with laughter. 'Oh

my goodness,' she added as she began to laugh. 'Dear oh me,' as she sat down in her chair. 'Children, children,' she said as the class roared. 'Where did you get it from, George?' she gasped.

But George was flopping over one arm of his wheelchair and Lizzie was dashing down the corridor to the toilet as fast as she could go.

'You can't take this around the whole school, George,' said Miss Baxter. 'It'll exhaust you.'

'I'll be all right,' said George, taking the bagged-up bird. 'I'll wait for Lizzie in the corridor.'

'Thank you, George,' said Miss Baxter. 'That's one bird the class will never forget.'

'Where next?' asked Lizzie running back to George.

'Let's take it to Mrs Stewart in the kitchen,' said George. 'I can hear the next class singing "Waltzing Matilda". They'll get to the nice sad slow bit soon and we don't want to spoil that – yet,' he said.

'Hello, children. What can I do for you?'
said kind Mrs Stewart as Lizzie pushed
George's wheelchair through the kitchen
door.

'I've got a surprise for you,' shouted
George and everybody in the kitchen
stopped work.

George pulled the kookaburra out of its
bag with a great flourish.

'What an evil-looking bird,' said Mrs
Stewart. 'Look – it's got its beak open just
like that dreadful Emu on the TV.'

'You pull the string at the back,' said
George. 'You try.'

Mrs Stewart pulled.

Lizzie sat down quickly on the tiled
floor.

And the bird began.

Soon the kitchen staff were sagging
over the sausages and bending over the
beans.

'TAKE IT AWAY!' shouted Mrs
Stewart. 'It'll be the death of us. Oh,
George – you terror. What will you do
next?'

So George pulled the string again and
Mrs Stewart staggered to a chair and

wiped her eyes with a roll of kitchen paper, waiting for the noise to stop.

'It's a kookaburra or laughing jackass from Australia,' said George parcelling it up.

'Then you won't catch me going to Australia,' said Mrs Stewart. 'How can anyone get on with their day's work with one of those crazy birds in the back garden?'

Lizzie sat for a moment getting her breath back. 'Are there really birds like that in the gardens there?' she asked.

'And spiders the size of your hand,' said Mrs Stewart.

'Then I'll go there when I grow up,' said Lizzie.

'Off you go now and take that fowl with you,' said Mrs Stewart.

'Goodbye,' said George. 'We'll go and cheer up the "Waltzing Matilda" class. But Lizzie can stay outside because she's all weak and wobbly.'

'No, I'm not,' said Lizzie. 'You're all right because you've got a wheelchair to sit in.'

'Oh, get along you two,' said Mrs

Stewart. 'I'm beginning to think of that tiresome bird again. And there's work to be done.'

That evening George and Lizzie were sitting in the playground with the kookaburra back in its bag when George's mother came to fetch him.

'Sorry, Mum,' said George. 'It got pulled too much. It won't work any more.'

'Oh well. Never mind,' said his mother. And Lizzie thought she did not sound sad at all. 'Did Lizzie like it?'

George nodded. 'She wanted to take it home to see if her dad can fix it.'

'Well, she can on one condition,' said George's mother. 'That it stays there and doesn't come back!'

## 3 Snow

One morning Lizzie and Dad plodded to school through deep snow and met Mr Gann, the caretaker, at the school gate.

'Nothing doing today, Lizzie,' said Mr Gann. 'The heating's broken down. I knew it would.'

'So the school's shut?' asked Dad.

Mr Gann nodded. 'It was on the local radio at seven-thirty. But nobody seems to have heard it. Morning, everybody,' he went on as another group of children arrived. 'School's shut today. The heating's off.'

All the parents looked at each other.

'Now what do I do?' said Samantha's mother. 'I'm on duty today. I have to go to work.'

'I'll take Samantha home with me, if you like,' Dad offered.

'D'you think you could have Ranjit?' asked Mr Ram. 'My wife's gone out already.'

'Yes, why not? The more the merrier,' said Dad.

'Good,' said Lizzie. 'Let's ask James and Rosie and Josh too.'

And she did.

Some time later, Lizzie and Dad arrived back home with six cheerful children.

Mum met them at the door. 'The electricity's gone off,' she said. Then she looked at all the children.

'There was nothing else for it,' Dad explained. 'There are lots of fish fingers in the freezer, aren't there?'

'We can't open the freezer while the electricity's off,' said Mum.

'Don't worry,' said Lizzie putting her arms around Mum's waist. 'They can have baked beans and spaghetti.'

'Oh well,' said Mum. 'Let's get their wet clothes off, and I'll light a fire in the sitting-room.'

'Can I get something from the shop before I go?' Dad asked.

'No, don't worry, we'll cope,' said Mum, kissing him goodbye.

'And I'll look after Fred for you, Mrs Jones,' said Samantha. 'No problem.'

'Thank you, Samantha,' said Mum.

While Mum lit a fire, the children ran upstairs and downstairs and into Lizzie's bedroom and into the larder and under the kitchen table. Suddenly Joshua and Rosie collided on the stairs and fell down together – bump – bump – yell! they went.

Mum clapped her hands loudly.

'Enough chasing about,' she said. 'You're all warmed up, so get a cushion from the sitting-room and come and sit on the kitchen floor – quietly.'

'What are we going to do?' Lizzie asked.

'Something,' said Mum. 'Something
quiet,' she added.

Gradually the children settled down on
the kitchen floor and looked hopefully at
Lizzie's mum.

Mum was thinking hard. Suddenly her
face lit up.

'Well done, Mum!' said Lizzie.

'I know,' Mum said. 'Work – that's it.
Much more fun than just playing about
and – perhaps – you'll get paid. All right?'

'Yes, yes,' shouted Rosie. 'I'm good at
working.'

Mum went to a cupboard and got out

two dusters and a tin of polish.

'Rosie and Joshua,' she said. 'Your job is to give all the wooden furniture a good polish. It's been lucky to get dusted since Fred was born.

Rosie and Joshua jumped up, took the dusters and polish, and went to make a start on the sitting-room.

'Now, Ranjit,' said Mum, handing him a broom. 'I want you to sweep the kitchen floor and Lizzie can use the dustpan. Then you can wipe down the cupboard fronts. All right?'

So Ranjit and Lizzie set to work.

'James and Samantha,' said Mum, putting some saucepans of water on the gas stove. 'We'll heat up some water and give Fred a bath in the big kitchen bowl by the sitting-room fire. How about that?'

Samantha nodded and rushed off upstairs. 'I'll get his clothes. Can I choose them?' she shouted.

'Yes,' called back Mum. 'And bring some soap and a flannel, please. Oh, another thing, children. Don't rush your jobs. We've got all day.'

Soon everybody was hard at work. The house began to smell of polish and shampoo. Rosie and Joshua moved upstairs to polish the wardrobe in the big bedroom and Ranjit set about washing the kitchen floor with the sponge on a long handle. Lizzie stood on the dry bits of floor pretending they were islands while the sea got closer and closer. Then Mum put down sheets of newspaper so that the children could jump from one sheet to another without stepping on the wet floor.

'Lizzie's mum said we'd get paid,'

James whispered to Samantha as he put
Fred's dirty clothes in the laundry
basket.

'Yes, but we mustn't ask because that's
rude,' Samantha whispered back.

Just at that moment Mum called. 'All
workers into the kitchen please. It's pay
time.'

All the workers came running and
stood on the newspaper islands.

'Now,' said Mum, opening the larder
door. 'There's a satsuma for all good

workers, a coffee for me and a rusk for Fred.'

'What about Scruffy?' asked Joshua, looking at Lizzie's big dog who was sitting patiently on a newspaper island.

'Scruffy can have a rusk too,' said Mum. 'I think she likes them better than Fred does.'

'And can we watch television?' Lizzie asked.

'Yes – no – there's no electricity. The television isn't working,' said Mum remembering.

'Never mind,' said Joshua. 'I'll be the television. I'll be the man on *Blue Peter*.'

'What can I be?' Rosie asked.

'You can be the lady who makes things,' said Joshua.

'I'll be a pop group,' said Samantha.

So they all settled down to watch Joshua fall off the kitchen stool, pretending he was jumping out of an aeroplane with a parachute. Scruffy ran out of the kitchen in a fright. Then Lizzie played the saucepan lids like cymbals while Samantha danced and sang using a spoon for a microphone.

Mum put her hands over her ears.

Suddenly Scruffy barked.

'Who's that? Oh good,' said Mum as Dad came in through the front door.

'Are you lot being good?' he asked.

'They're being marvellous,' said Mum. 'They've done the housework.'

'Excellent,' said Dad. 'And this afternoon I'll take them all tobogganing and then they can come back and sweep the chimney. How about that?'

'No, no,' yelled Lizzie. 'We'll get all sooty and there's *no hot water*.'

'Then I'll roll you in the snow,' said Dad. 'And another thing,' he said, feeling in his pocket. 'Here are some batteries for the kitchen radio. We don't want to miss tomorrow's school announcements on the local radio, do we? Or we might get you lot again!'

# 4 Running Away

Lizzie and Ranjit were playing together one morning when Ranjit said, 'My mum's not well.'

Lizzie nodded and carried on pushing a toy car along a white line on the playground.

'My dad's had to go to Birmingham today. She's all by herself,' Ranjit went on.

'Where's Birmingham?' asked Lizzie.

'I don't know,' said Ranjit. 'I don't like it when my mum's ill.'

'No,' said Lizzie. And she remembered a time when her mother had stayed in bed and Fred had cried all the time. 'No, it's horrid,' she said.

'I'm going to see if she's all right,' said Ranjit suddenly and he turned and ran off towards the school gates.

Lizzie ran after him. 'You're not allowed to go out,' she shouted. 'You'll get into trouble.'

But Ranjit just ran on over the grass and through the gate, turning left and dashing away up towards his house.

Lizzie stood watching Ranjit disappear. Then she turned and looked back at the teacher who was on playtime duty. But the teacher was bending over a girl who had fallen over and she had not seen Ranjit run away.

Lizzie walked back towards the classroom just as the whistle blew for the end of playtime. Everybody lined up and went indoors to start on their workbooks.

One by one the children went up to Mrs Armstrong's desk to practise their

reading. Ranjit always had his turn
before Lizzie, so, when Mrs Armstrong
called, 'Ranjit, reading time,' Lizzie went
up instead, hoping she wouldn't notice
the difference.

But she did.

'Where's Ranjit?' she asked in surprise.

'He's gone,' said Lizzie.

'Gone where?' asked Mrs Armstrong in
a puzzled voice.

'Just gone – home,' said Lizzie

unhappily.

'But why?' asked Mrs Armstrong.

'Because his mum's ill and his dad's gone to Birmingham,' Lizzie explained.

'Oh dear,' said Mrs Armstrong, standing up. 'Now, children,' she said. 'Get on with your work quietly. I must tell Miss Thompson what's happened. I'll be back in a moment.'

A little later Mrs Armstrong came back looking worried.

'Is Ranjit all right, Mrs Armstrong?' Samantha asked. 'He shouldn't go out on the road by himself, should he?' she said.

'No, of course he shouldn't,' said Mrs Armstrong. 'Get on with your work, Samantha.'

'Did he get home all right?' asked Lizzie

'Well, no. We just don't know. We've tried to telephone his mother but there's no answer,' said Mrs Armstrong.

Lizzie felt frightened. 'I didn't stop him. Will he get run over?' she said.

'No, I'm sure he won't,' said Mrs Armstrong. 'But it's always right to tell the teacher on duty when something like that happens. Mrs Crespi is walking along to his house to look for him.'

Lizzie tried to get on with her reading but Mrs Armstrong had to help her with a lot more words than usual. 'Don't worry, Lizzie,' she said kindly. 'Ranjit's a sensible boy. He'll be all right.'

'But it wasn't sensible to go out by himself, was it, Mrs Armstrong?' said Samantha.

'No, dear, it wasn't. Now let's do your reading, Samantha. You're on the rabbit that went hop, chop, lop, flop, aren't you?' said Mrs Armstrong.

At dinner time Lizzie saw Mrs Crespi, the school secretary, sitting in her office. She went and tapped on the glass panel and Mrs Crespi pushed it back.

'Please, is Ranjit all right?' Lizzie asked. 'Did he get run over?' she added.

'No. He's quite all right, love,' said Mrs Crespi. 'But his mother is really very poorly. She couldn't answer the telephone. But Ranjit let me into the house and I rang for the doctor straight away.'

'What did the doctor say?' Lizzie asked.

'Well, her next-door neighbour,
Harinder's mother, came round to be
with her so that I could come back here.
So I don't know what the doctor said,
love.'

Lizzie nodded.

'Cheer up,' said Mrs Crespi. 'I'm sure
things will work out all right.'

When Lizzie's mum arrived at school that
afternoon Lizzie ran out to meet her.

'What's the matter?' Mum said when she saw Lizzie's face.

'Ranjit's mother's ill,' Lizzie said. 'Ranjit ran away. But he didn't get run over.'

'Well, I'm glad to hear that,' said Mum. 'What's wrong with his mother?'

Lizzie shook her head. 'I don't know. But his dad's gone to Birmingham.'

'I can see why Ranjit was worried,' said Mum.

'Can we go and see him – please?' said Lizzie. 'He ran away at playtime. I didn't tell anyone.'

'You should have done,' said Mum. 'He might have got into trouble. But yes, all right. We'll go and see him.'

And she turned Fred's pushchair to the left as they went out of the school gates.

But there was no answer when they rang the bell of Ranjit's house a few minutes later.

'Harinder lives next door,' said Lizzie. 'Let's try her house.'

It was Harinder's elder brother who opened the door to them.

Suddenly Ranjit appeared in the

hallway too.

'Hello, Lizzie,' he shouted. 'My mum's gone to hospital. She might have her appendix out.'

'Oh, poor Mrs Ram,' said Mum. 'I am sorry. When will your father be home, Ranjit?'

'I think he'll be home late tonight,' Harinder's brother answered for him. 'The children can stay here in the meantime.'

'I wish I could help somehow,' said Mum. 'What can I do?'

Lizzie pulled at her coat. 'I know,' she said. 'Ranjit can come and stay at our house. He can sleep on my bed and I can sleep on the li-lo.'

Then Lizzie saw Ranjit's little sister tottering down the hall towards them and she sighed. 'And I suppose she can come too,' she said.

Mum stepped inside and spoke to Harinder's mother. Ranjit and Lizzie watched them discussing how long Mrs Ram might be in hospital and what would be best for the children.

In the end Mum said, 'Look, I'll leave a

note for Mr Ram saying I'll gladly have Ranjit to stay if he would like it. But he'll have a shock when he hears his wife's in hospital and Ranjit will want to be with him at first, won't he?'

Ranjit nodded. 'Can I go and see my mum in hospital?' he asked.

'Yes, of course, dear,' said Mum. 'And tomorrow I'll telephone Harinder's mother to find out what Mr Ram wants to do. All right?'

As they walked home it was getting dark and they didn't talk much.

Suddenly Lizzie said, 'It was a good thing Ranjit went home to see if his mother was all right.'

'Yes, I suppose it was,' said Mum.

'But it was a bad thing too, wasn't it?' said Lizzie.

'Well, yes, I suppose it was,' said Mum again.

They walked along quietly for some while until Mum said, 'I had my appendix out years ago, by the way. So you stay safely inside the school gates. Understand? No running home just to check.'

'No, I won't,' laughed Lizzie.

The next day Ranjit came home from
school with Lizzie and stayed at her
house for five nights.

He brought a plastic bag with his
pyjamas and some clean socks and pants,
and a note about what food he ate.

And he played a lot with Fred in the
evenings and said he wished his sister
was as funny.

But Lizzie said she preferred Ranjit's
sister who was quiet and shy – and at
Harinder's house.

# 5 Spilt Milk

'Are you listening, children?' Mrs Armstrong asked one morning.

'Yes, Mrs Armstrong,' said the children, sitting very still.

'Next week, children, we have a very important job to do. It is our turn to decorate the entrance hall for the next half of term. And we're going to do it with a huge Spring picture. Now, put up your hands if you have any ideas for our

Spring picture. Yes, Samantha?' said Mrs
Armstrong.

'Daffodils,' said Samantha.

'That's right. And lots of other Spring
flowers too,' said Mrs Armstrong.

'Lambs and chicks,' said Lizzie.

'Cygnets,' said Joshua. 'There are some
on the river near us. They're baby
swans,' he explained.

'Well done, Joshua,' said Mrs
Armstrong.

'Easter eggs and chocolate rabbits,'
shouted Samantha, and all the other
children agreed at once.

And so, every afternoon for the next week, the children worked away at the Spring picture.

Mrs Armstrong covered one wall of the entrance hall with smooth paper and Lizzie and Harinder painted the bottom half green for the grass and, standing on solid chairs from the Wendy House, they painted the top half blue for the sky.

Meanwhile the rest of the class painted yellow chicks and white, brown and black lambs. They cut them out and stuck them on the green grass. Polly brought in some real sheep's wool which she had found on the wire around a field near her home, and she stuck that on some of the lambs to make them more real.

Samantha painted some yellow daffodils straight on to the grass and gave some of them orange middles.

Joshua painted a blue pond on the grass and stuck his swan and cygnets on to that. And one morning he arrived with a lot of tiny twigs in a plastic bag. He stuck those next to the pond to make a nest for his swans.

Gradually the picture got better and

better and Miss Thompson, the head teacher, admired it every time she went past.

But Lizzie had thought of something.

'Mrs Armstrong,' she said, putting up her hand just before story time. 'It rains a lot in the Spring, doesn't it?'

Mrs Armstrong nodded. 'Sometimes it even snows,' she said.

'So can I paint some grey clouds and raindrops in the sky, please – tomorrow?' Lizzie asked.

'All right, Lizzie. I'll mix some grey paint for you. Now, when everyone is sitting still, I'll start the story.'

The next afternoon Mrs Armstrong helped Lizzie into her overall and, carrying a chair and small table from the Wendy House, went with her down the corridor to the entrance hall. She put a pot of grey paint on the table and watched as Lizzie stepped up on to the chair.

'We'll be getting on with our Spring writing,' she told Lizzie. 'Bring the paint back to the classroom when you've finished. It shouldn't take you long.'

'All right, Mrs Armstrong,' said Lizzie happily. 'See you later.'

Very carefully, trying not to let the paint run too much, Lizzie began to paint a great billowing rain cloud. Then dot, dot, dot she went to show the rain drops falling on the grass.

Lizzie got down off the chair and stood back to admire her work. She *was* pleased.

Hopping back up on the chair again she leant sideways to start another cloud.

And then it happened.

Her knee knocked the edge of the table and, thud, the jar of grey paint fell over, shooting paint on the edge of the Spring picture before it fell off the table and rolled gently away towards the main doors.

Lizzie stared in horror. There was a huge splodge of grey paint all over Samantha's yellow daffodils. Pulling off her overall she used it to rub at the paint. But it was no good. She just made it worse. Tears welled up and blocked her nose. She picked up the paint jar and ran

back down the corridor. Seeing the door
of Mr Gann's cupboard standing ajar she
darted inside and began to cry.

'What's all this?' said a voice at the
door as the cupboard light went on. 'Has
the sky fallen down?' asked Mr Gann
putting a tin of varnish down on the
shelf.

Lizzie nodded miserably. 'I've spoilt the
Spring picture. I didn't mean to. I'm
sorry.'

'Oh dear, oh dear. Come along, missie. Let's see the damage.'

Together Lizzie and Mr Gann walked back to the entrance hall. Lizzie looked at the great grey patch. It was just as bad as she had thought.

Mr Gann looked at it too. 'The best thing for you to do is to own up at once,' he said. 'These things get worse if you leave them.'

'But those daffodils are Samantha's and she'll be all cross and horrid – I know she will,' said Lizzie.

Mr Gann nodded. 'Probably,' he said. 'How about me coming with you? Then I can see you being brave.'

So they walked back down to the quiet classroom where everybody was busy.

Mrs Armstrong looked up from Polly's writing and said, 'Whatever's the matter, Lizzie?'

'I've knocked over the grey paint all down the Spring picture and it's all spoilt and so – and so are Samantha's daffodils,' said Lizzie in a rush.

'Ow – ow,' began Samantha in a wailing voice and, jumping up, she ran past Lizzie and down the corridor.

Lizzie, Mrs Armstrong and Mr Gann walked after her.

'Well,' said Mrs Armstrong when they stood in front of the picture. 'It could be worse. It's only that corner that's caught it.'

Lizzie went over to Samantha who was crouched over the disaster area. 'Sorry,' she said. 'I didn't mean to.'

Samantha rubbed at the mess with her finger. Suddenly she stopped and looking

round at Lizzie she said, 'It's no good crying over spilt milk.'

Mrs Armstrong gasped. 'Samantha,' she said. 'Where did you hear that?'

'Yesterday,' said Samantha. 'I dropped a bottle of milk on the kitchen floor and my mum got mad and then she said "It's no good crying over spilt milk." Then she was all right again.'

'Well,' said Mrs Armstrong, giving Samantha a hug. 'You've got a very wise mother. Hasn't she, Lizzie?'

Lizzie glowed with relief. 'Yes, yes,' she said, hugging Samantha too. 'And anyway,' she added brightly, 'they weren't very good daffodils, were they? They were a bit . . .'

'Lizzie,' said Mrs Armstrong sharply, 'run along and get a bucket of water. This mess must be cleared up.'

Late that afternoon Mrs Armstrong found Ranjit sitting on the floor in the entrance hall staring at the grey splodge.

'I'm waiting for my father,' he explained. Then he added, 'I think that grey paint looks like an elephant.'

Mrs Armstrong squatted down beside him. 'Yes,' she said. 'I see what you mean, that long streak could be his trunk.'

Ranjit nodded. 'My grandmother told me about an elephant. It came to her village in India in the Spring. And it was painted all over. It had stripes and loops and dots. And, do you know?'

'What?' said Mrs Armstrong.

'It was as tall as a house,' said Ranjit.

And then he looked at Mrs Armstrong and Mrs Armstrong looked at him and they both laughed.

'Go ahead, Ranjit,' she said. 'Tomorrow you can change that splodge into your Spring elephant. Just think how pleased Lizzie will be.'

'So will my grandmother,' said Ranjit. 'I'll get her to draw me a picture. And I think it had shiny mirror bits down its trunk. Can we do those too?'

'And could Samantha help you?' Mrs Armstrong asked.

'All right,' said Ranjit. 'She can put Easter eggs on its back. That'll please her!'